Bantam Books in the Choose Your Own Adventure® Series
Ask your bookseller for the books you have missed

Choose Your Own Adventure® Books for younger readers

CHOOSE YOUR OWN ADVENTURE® • 9

WHO KILLED HARLOWE THROMBEY?

BY EDWARD PACKARD

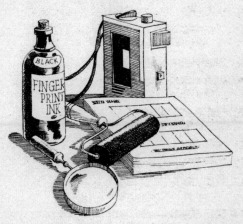

ILLUSTRATED BY PAUL GRANGER

BANTAM BOOKS
TORONTO · NEW YORK · LONDON · SYDNEY

RL 5, IL age 10 and up

WHO KILLED HARLOWE THROMBEY?

A Bantam Book / February 1981

2nd printing .... April 1981	5th printing ..... January 1982
3rd printing .... June 1981	6th printing ..... February 1982
4th printing ..... January 1982	7th printing .... March 1982
8th printing ...... August 1982	

Original Conception of Edward Packard

Illustrated by Paul Granger

CHOOSE YOUR OWN ADVENTURE ® is a
trademark of Bantam Books, Inc.

ISBN 0-553-23181-2

Published simultaneously in the United States and Canada

Bantam Books are published by Bantam Books, Inc. Its trademark, consisting of the words "Bantam Books" and the por-
trayal of a rooster, is Registered in U.S. Patent and Trademark
Office and in other countries. Marca Registrada. Bantam
Books, Inc., 666 Fifth Avenue, New York, New York 10103.

PRINTED IN THE UNITED STATES OF AMERICA

O   17   16   15   14   13   12   11   10   9   8

WARNING!!!!

Do not read this book straight through from beginning to end! These pages contain many different experiences you can have while working as a detective. From time to time as you read along, you will be asked to make a choice. After you make your choice, follow the instructions to see what happens to you next.

Your success in solving the Harlowe Thrombey murder mystery will depend a lot on *your* decisions. Some leads will bring you closer to the answer; others will throw you off the track.

Think carefully before you make each move! There could be danger waiting for you at every turn. Try to catch the murderer before the murderer catches you.

Good luck!

2

It's been just a year since the robber climbed in your Aunt Marinda's bedroom window at two o'clock in the morning.

"Get out!" she screamed at him, and that's just what he did, taking her pearl necklace with him.

The next day you found a beer bottle in the bushes outside Aunt Marinda's house. Since she isn't the sort to toss beer bottles out the window, you handed it over to the police.

The robber's fingerprints were on the bottle, the police quickly identified him, and now he's safely behind bars.

Since then, you've gotten quite a reputation as a detective. You've equipped yourself with a magnifying glass, fingerprint kit and a cassette recorder, and you're ready for business.

Some of your friends have decided to become detectives too. That's O.K. They're just a bunch of amateurs, except maybe for that frizzy-haired girl down the street—Jenny Mudge. She's definitely smart. In fact, sometimes you think she might be smarter than you are.

Now it looks like you've got your first big case. Harlowe Thrombey, President of Thrombey Plastics Company, has just called and asked you to come to his house at five o'clock this afternoon.

"I hear you have sharp eyes," he said. "And that's what I need right now. I think my life is in danger."

Go on to page 4.

You asked Thrombey what he was afraid of, but he didn't want to talk on the phone, so you said you'd think about it and call back.

It was exciting to get a call from Harlowe Thrombey. But maybe you should find out more about him before taking the case.

If you phone Thrombey and accept his invitation, turn to page 5.

If you tell him that you can't come this afternoon, but you'll call him back in a day or so, turn to page 17.

You knock on Thrombey's door exactly at five. A stout, balding man opens it. He eyes you suspiciously before nervously shaking your hand.

"I'm Harlowe Thrombey," he says. "Before we go inside, I'll show you around the place."

The two of you stroll across the lawn past scores of flowering shrubs and trees. Ahead of you is a large greenhouse.

"Why do you think your life is in danger?" you ask.

"It's my wife, Jane," Thrombey says. "I do everything to make her happy—expensive cars, trips around the world. She even has two pianos—a concert grand for herself and a smaller one for guests." He stops in his tracks and turns toward you, a dark look on his face. "The truth is, I think she would rather have me dead."

Go on to page 6.

"What makes you think that?"

Thrombey pauses again before replying. "She told me."

A few steps further, reaching the greenhouse, you watch curiously as Thrombey rattles the door and then turns toward you again.

"I wanted to make sure it was locked for the night," he says. "Jenkins, our gardener, keeps arsenic there for spraying the trees. The poor fellow's laid up in the hospital."

"Maybe your wife just lost her temper," you suggest.

"I'd like to think so," Thrombey says, shaking his head. "Maybe you'll be able to judge when you meet her. She's playing in a concert this afternoon and should be back by six."

As you are walking back to the front entrance to the house, Thrombey points at a bright red sports car pulling up to a stop. A trim, bearded man gets out and starts toward you.

Go on to the next page.

"That's Dr. Robert Lipscomb," Thrombey says. "He's coming for dinner tonight, along with my nephew, Chartwell, and my niece, Angela. I think Angela and Robert are planning to marry. I want to get to know Robert better, so I asked him to come early and play a few games of pool. Do you want to join us, or would you rather take a look around the place? There's no one here but Helga, our cook."

If you decide to look around the place,
turn to page 8.

If you decide to play pool with Harlowe
Thrombey and Dr. Robert Lipscomb,
turn to page 12.

You walk through the rear hall and into the pantry, where you hear voices coming from the kitchen. A woman and a young girl are talking.

"Do you really think Mr. Thrombey's life is in danger?" the girl asks.

"I don't know," the woman replies, "but I've seen his niece, Angela, snooping through his papers, and his nephew, Chartwell, prowling about the grounds."

Stepping around the corner, you meet a tiny, blond-haired woman wearing a white blouse and blue-checkered apron. Standing next to her—much to your surprise—is Jenny Mudge.

"Hi. What are you doing here?" says Jenny.

"Mr. Thrombey asked me over," you reply. "What are *you* doing here?"

"Oh . . . have you met Helga?" Jenny says. "I'm in her cooking class at the 'Y' and I invited myself over to see her kitchen and learn how to make my favorite chocolate cake."

As you introduce yourself to Helga, Jenny glances at her watch. "My gosh, it's six o'clock. I have to get home. Thanks, Helga." She hurries out the back door. "See you later!" she calls over her shoulder.

You wonder whether Jenny came to learn cooking, or to do detective work! Walking back toward the game room, you find Harlowe Thrombey standing in the hall, a puzzled look on his face.

"I ended up playing pool alone," he says. "Robert said he had to make some phone calls in the library. But he's not there now."

As Thrombey is speaking, the front door opens, and Robert walks in. Behind him is

Thrombey's tall, stoop-shouldered nephew, Chartwell.

"I noticed Chartwell's car in the driveway," Robert explains, "but he didn't come in, so I went out to meet him."

Chartwell gives Robert a curious look and then shakes your hand as Thrombey introduces you.

Turn to page 10.

Thrombey shows Robert, Chartwell, and you into the library just as the grandfather clock in the hall strikes six. Glancing out the window, you see a white Cadillac pulling up the drive.

"That's Jane," Thrombey says, "back from her concert."

A few moments later, a large, round-faced woman enters the library.

"So pleased to meet you," Jane says, shaking your hand. "I've heard a lot about you. Will you be joining us for dinner?"

Thrombey's wife is surprisingly friendly. It's hard to see why he should be afraid of her. Maybe he just imagines his life is in danger. You don't want to sit through a boring dinner, especially since there's a very good movie you'd like to catch at home on TV. You glance at Harlowe Thrombey.

"Do stay, if you'd like," he says.

If you accept the invitation for dinner, turn to page 13.

If you tell Thrombey you can't stay but you'll talk to him tomorrow, turn to page 17.

The game has hardly begun when Robert leaves to use the phone in the library, explaining that he has to check on one of his patients in the hospital. He returns about twenty minutes later just as the doorbell rings.

"That must be Chartwell," Thrombey says.

You and Robert go with Thrombey to the front door, where he introduces you to his nephew, Chartwell, a tall, stoop-shouldered young man.

Turn to page 10.

Jane leaves to dress for dinner. When she rejoins the rest of you in the library it's almost seven o'clock.

"Does anyone know where Angela is?" she asks.

There is no response, but a moment later the question is answered by a knock on the door. Thrombey opens it and a slender young woman steps inside. Her very light skin contrasts with her dark hair and eyes and her black velvet dress.

"Angela, at last you're here," Thrombey says.

"Sorry to be late. I was at my dentist in Springdale. It's almost an hour's drive from here," says Angela.

"That's all right, my dear," says Thrombey. "Now that you're here, I'll ask Helga to serve dinner. She wants to leave early to visit Jenkins, our gardener, in the hospital."

In a few moments everyone is seated around the large oak dining table. Helga brings in salad, rolls, and a platter of roast beef, which Harlowe Thrombey carves with a long silver knife. The roast tastes as good as it looks, but everyone seems tense and nervous, and you can hardly enjoy the meal.

After dinner, Helga clears off the dishes and hurries out the door. A few minutes later, at about eight o'clock, Thrombey offers his guests brandy. Everyone but you accepts, and he goes to the pantry, returning a few minutes later with five glasses on a tray.

"I find a glass of brandy before bed helps me sleep," Thrombey says, "and, of course, it's good after dinner, too. . . ."

Turn to page 15.

"Here's to good health and long life, sir," Robert says, as he raises his glass, and the others join in the drinking. Then Robert, Chartwell, and Harlowe Thrombey leave for the game room to play pool, while Angela follows Jane into the music room. Thrombey asks you to join them in the game room. You'd rather play pool, but your job, after all, is to watch Jane.

The music room is half-filled by two grand pianos. Jane sits at one and Angela at the other, while you relax in an armchair.

"I'm so glad to hear you're taking piano lessons," Jane says to Angela. "Would you like to play a duet with me?"

"Oh no, you're so much better. I'd rather listen to you," Angela replies.

Jane smiles at the compliment as she loudly strikes the first notes of Beethoven's *Moonlight Sonata*.

You listen patiently for half an hour, until about 8:30, then slip out of the room and go to the library where you spend about twenty minutes looking at Thrombey's collection of books and hunting trophies. Leaving the library, you can still hear the piano, so you walk down the hall to the game room. Chartwell and Robert are playing pool, but Harlowe Thrombey is not with them.

Suddenly you hear a terrifying scream. Rushing to the hall, you are shocked to see Harlowe Thrombey lurching toward you. He falls and lies moaning on the floor. The others come running. Robert dashes to Thrombey's side. Jane starts to cry. Angela and Chartwell stand helplessly nearby. You run to the library and telephone for an ambulance. It takes a few minutes to get the call through. You rush back to Thrombey, and stare a moment at his ashen gray face, then kneel down beside him.

"I've been poisoned," he gasps.

"Do you know who did it?"

For a moment, he struggles to get up, then falls back. Clutching at his throat, he whispers, "It . . . it . . . was . . ." But those are his last words.

You rush to the pantry where you find the open brandy bottle. Your watch reads 9:03. From experience, you know you may be able to learn more *before* the police arrive than afterward. You must work quickly.

If you decide to talk to the witnesses one at a time, turn to page 19.

If you decide to talk to them as a group, turn to page 20.

The next morning you're up early, thinking about Harlowe Thrombey—wondering whether his life really is in danger. Your thoughts are interrupted by the ringing telephone. A shaking voice is on the wire.

"This is John McGee, Harlowe Thrombey's lawyer. Have you heard the news?"

"What news?"

"Mr. Thrombey told me that if anything happened to him, I was to call you. I'm afraid something *has* happened! Harlowe Thrombey has been murdered! He was poisoned last night. Someone broke into the greenhouse about six o'clock and took a bottle of arsenic. Later, the murderer poured the arsenic into Thrombey's brandy bottle."

"How awful," you reply. "He told me his life was in danger, but I hardly believed him. . . ."

"None of us did," McGee says. "The police seem to think his wife, Jane, did it, but I would bet it was one of the dinner guests."

"Who were they?" you ask.

"His nephew, Chartwell; his niece, Angela; and her boyfriend, Dr. Robert Lipscomb."

"Let me ask you another question," you continue. "Do the police know when the murderer poured the arsenic into Thrombey's brandy bottle?"

"Not exactly," McGee says, "but they know it must have been between eight o'clock, when he gave his guests a drink, and nine o'clock, when he went back to pour another for himself."

Go on to page 18.

"And how do they know the greenhouse was broken into about six o'clock?"

"That was quite a stroke of luck," McGee says. "A young girl was visiting Helga, the Thrombeys' cook. She noticed the greenhouse was locked at four o'clock when she came to visit and that when she left at six o'clock it had been broken open."

"She must have sharp eyes," you say.

"You may know her," McGee says. "Jenny Mudge is her name."

You thank McGee for calling and hang up the phone. Shocked by the news, you resolve to do your best to solve the Harlowe Thrombey murder case. From what you know of Jenny Mudge, you can be sure she has the same idea.

Inspector Prufrock will be in charge of the case, no doubt. In your opinion he is a bumbling idiot. Even with the whole police force working for him, he usually can't solve the simplest of cases. Still, it would be a good idea to talk to him and find out whether he has stumbled across anything important. On the other hand, perhaps you should first inspect the scene of the crime.

If you go to police headquarters to talk to Inspector Prufrock, turn to page 23.

If you go to the Thrombey house, turn to page 26.

You decide to interview as many of the witnesses as you can, one at a time, until the police arrive. You'd also like to inspect the pantry before the police disturb it.

If you interview:

Chartwell, turn to page 27.

Robert, turn to page 28.

Angela, turn to page 29.

Jane, turn to page 30.

If, instead, you inspect the pantry, turn to page 31.

Before you have time to ask any questions, Chartwell tries to take over.

"My uncle and I often fought," he says angrily, "but I'm going to find out who murdered him if it's the last thing I do!"

"Just a moment," Robert says. "Let's be calm. There's no need for an investigation! Thrombey told me who the murderer was the moment I reached him."

"What did he say?" you ask.

"He was very weak; he could hardly talk," Robert replies, "but I distinctly heard him say, *'It was Jane. She poured my last drink!'* "

"You liar!" Jane shouts.

Everyone begins talking at once, and it takes you a moment to quiet them down.

"I want to know where *everyone* was between the time Thrombey served brandy and the time he went back to pour his last drink."

"Actually," Chartwell says, "Robert and I never left the game room."

You are interrupted by a loud knocking at the door. In a moment, Police Inspector Prufrock and two officers storm into the room.

"Everyone stay where you are!" Prufrock shouts.

Turn to page 34.

You find Prufrock, a bald man with a huge black mustache, sitting at his desk, puffing on a long-stem pipe. On the walls of his office are pictures of famous criminals now behind bars.

"Well, well, the great detective is here," he says sarcastically. "I'm afraid you're a little late. I've solved the crime." He rises from his chair and gazes down at you. "Thrombey's wife, Jane, did it. She was the only one who knew he drank a glass of brandy every night before going to bed. Besides, Robert Lipscomb says that Thrombey's last words were *'Jane did it.'* "

Smiling with satisfaction, Prufrock points to the door. "So you see, my friend, it's just a matter of bringing Jane Thrombey in and getting her confession."

"That's great," you say, "but, if you don't mind, I'd like to check a few things out for myself."

"By all means," Prufrock says grandly. "Go ahead! Here, you can take a copy of the police report on the case."

Now, outside police headquarters, you consider how to begin your investigation.

According to the police report, all the dinner guests agreed that:

1. At 8:00, Helga, the cook, left to visit Jenkins, the gardener, in the hospital;
2. Right afterward, Thrombey served everyone brandy;
3. Shortly before 9:00, Thrombey poured himself the glass of poisoned brandy.

Go on to page 24.

4. Between eight o'clock and nine o'clock someone must have poured the arsenic into Thrombey's brandy bottle;

5. Thrombey's nephew, Chartwell, and Robert Lipscomb each say that they both stayed in the game room all evening and that Thrombey left them to go pour his last drink;

6. Thrombey's wife, Jane, and his niece, Angela, each claim to have spent the whole evening in the music room but insist that the other left for ten minutes. Jane says that she played the concert grand piano while Angela was out of the room, and Angela claims that she played the smaller piano while Jane was out of the room.

Go on to the next page.

When you return home, you find a note slipped under the door that reads:

> If you want to find out who murdered Harlowe Thrombey, go to the White Horse Inn and ask for a man named Falcon.

If you decide to check the police records for a man named Falcon, turn to page 47.

If you decide to go to the White Horse Inn and ask for a man named Falcon, turn to page 48.

When you arrive at the Thrombey house, you find no one home except Helga, the maid. A slight, shy woman with soft brown eyes, she tells you she spent from five o'clock until six o'clock with Jenny Mudge, cooking in the kitchen, and that she left after dinner at eight to visit her brother in the hospital, staying until nine.

"Do you have any idea who did it?" you ask.

"I've been trying to think," she replies. "I would guess it was Dr. Robert Lipscomb. There is something I don't like about that man! But I don't see how he could have done it, because Chartwell says that Robert stayed with him in the game room all evening, and I know Chartwell wouldn't lie to protect Robert. I once overheard him tell Mr. Thrombey that he didn't trust Robert."

You thank Helga for her information and go to the hospital, where you find that she did indeed visit Jenkins from 8:00 to 9:00 the night of the murder.

By this time, you're curious to know whether Jenny Mudge discovered anything.

Turn to page 41.

"My uncle and I never got along very well," Chartwell tells you, "but I would never murder anyone. And it's not true that I wanted to get control of Thrombey Plastics Company. Money and power don't interest me!"

"I understand," you say, "but right now I'm interested in the facts. Where were you when Harlowe Thrombey screamed?"

"In the game room! Robert and I were waiting for Harlowe to come back and finish the game."

"What did you do after dinner?"

"We were in the game room the whole time."

"We?"

"Me and Robert . . . and Harlowe—until he went out to the pantry for his last drink."

Suddenly, there is a commotion in the hall. The police have arrived, led by Inspector Prufrock.

Turn to page 34.

You walk down to the end of the hall with Robert so you can talk in private.

"If only I could have saved him," Robert says. "It was a heavy dose. I'm glad that I was able to hear his last words, terrible though they were."

"What were they?" you ask.

"It's so tragic. I hate to be the one who must point the finger of guilt, but . . . near the end, Harlowe said to me very clearly, '*Jane did it. She poured my drink!*' "

"Did he say anything else?"

"No," Robert replies. "He was very weak, and it was a great effort for him to talk at all."

Suddenly, there is a loud knocking on the door. A second later, two policemen stride in, led by Inspector Prufrock.

Turn to page 34.

As you walk with Angela down the hall, she turns and clutches at your arm.

"It's tragic. He was *such* a good man," she says. "We were very close friends. I shall be grateful if you can find out who murdered him."

"I'll do my best," you reply, "but I need your help. Tell me exactly what you did after I left the music room."

"Well . . . the truth is that I was in the music room the whole time. After you left, Jane asked me to play a piano duet with her, but almost as soon as we started she got up and left the room. I thought it was quite rude of her."

"How about you? Did you leave the room?"

"No . . . not until I heard poor Harlowe scream."

Angela bows her head and begins to sob. At the same time, the front door swings open. It's Inspector Prufrock with two policemen behind him.

Turn to page 34.

At first, Jane Thrombey seems almost too upset to talk.

"Harlowe thought I was out to get him, but I would never have done this!" she cries.

"It's a terrible blow," you say. "Tell me, though, where were you after I left the music room at 8:30?"

"Why, I continued playing the piano— Beethoven's *Moonlight Sonata.* Angela had said she wanted to hear it, but as soon as I started playing, she left the room. I thought it quite rude of her."

You are about to ask another question when you hear a noise in the hall. Police Inspector Prufrock has arrived.

Turn to page 34.

After asking the others to wait in the library, you start toward the pantry. Hearing someone following, you turn and find yourself face to face with Chartwell.

"Let's look for clues," he says eagerly.

You are about to ask him to return to the library when you are interrupted by loud voices from the front hall. Police Inspector Prufrock has arrived.

Turn to page 34.

You walk across the lawn, wet with the evening dew. When you reach the greenhouse, you are surprised to find the door wide open. You shine your pocket flashlight on the door frame and look at it through your magnifying glass. The wood looks as if it has been gouged by a large pair of sharp-pointed shears.

Inside, you walk past rows of potted plants. At the far end is a steel file cabinet. On the top shelf are bottles of insecticide and rat poison. The shelf is covered with dust except in one small round space from which a bottle has obviously been removed.

Suddenly a voice calls, "Who's there?"

It's Prufrock, shining his flashlight in your eyes. "Oh, it's you," he says. "We phoned Jenkins at the hospital. He says there's a bottle of arsenic on top of that cabinet."

"There isn't anymore," you reply. "Someone broke in this afternoon and took it."

"One thing we can be sure of, then," Prufrock says, "Jane Thrombey didn't do it. She had her own key and wouldn't have needed to force the door open." He stands silently for a moment, apparently thinking. "Well, the evidence is gone. There's nothing more to do tonight. I'm going home to get some sleep."

If you check further for fingerprints and other clues in the greenhouse, turn to page 37.

If you go back and check out the pantry, turn to page 40.

34

A big man with a bushy red mustache, Prufrock strides around the library like a drill sergeant.

"Be very careful about fingerprints," he says to his men in a loud voice, "and I want anything that looks suspicious sent to the lab for analysis."

"Yes, sir," the officers reply.

Prufrock asks everyone to identify himself, and starts making notes in a little black book. When he learns Robert Lipscomb is a physician, he looks up with a sly smile. "You must know a great deal about poisons, Doctor."

Robert flushes with anger. "Are you implying that I murdered Thrombey?" he cries.

Ignoring Robert, Prufrock says, "I'm going to talk to you one at a time, and remember—anything you say may be used against you. Robert Lipscomb, come with me. Officer Schmidt will stay with the rest of you."

Prufrock crosses the room and looks you in the eye. "So, the great detective is here," he says sarcastically. "You might as well go home to bed. I won't have any trouble solving this one."

You smile to yourself. It's not likely this will be the case that breaks Prufrock's long string of unsolved crimes. In any event, Thrombey asked for your help, and it's your duty to figure out who murdered him. While Prufrock questions the dinner guests, you decide to look elsewhere.

If you inspect the greenhouse, turn to page 33.

If you go to the hospital to talk to Jenkins, the gardener, turn to page 35.

It's past visiting hours, but you are able to get permission from Jenkins' doctor to see him. You reach his bedside about 10:00 P.M. and gently break the news about Thrombey's death.

"I know," Jenkins murmurs. "Inspector Prufrock just called me on the phone. He asked if there was a bottle of arsenic in the greenhouse and I told him there was."

"Who besides you knew that?"

Jenkins rubs his forehead. "Mr. and Mrs. Thrombey, of course, and Chartwell. He was always snooping around whenever he came to visit. And Angela. She loved gardening."

"What about Dr. Robert Lipscomb?"

"I don't believe he's visited the house more than once or twice, and I never saw him near the greenhouse."

Jenkins falls back on his pillow, obviously exhausted. You thank him for his help and call it a night.

Go on to page 36.

Next morning you're up early, hopeful that by the end of the day you will have solved the Harlowe Thrombey murder case. You've hardly finished breakfast when the phone rings. It's Jenny Mudge.

"I've been working on the Harlowe Thrombey murder case," she says, "and I think we ought to have a talk about it. Could you come over to my house?"

If you tell Jenny you think it's more important for you to investigate at the Thrombey house instead, turn to page 39.

If you agree to meet Jenny at her house, turn to page 41.

If you just sit for a few minutes to think things through, turn to page 42.

You take some fingerprint impressions. Most of them are of the same person—probably Jenkins, the gardener. But you find another man's thumb and fingerprint on a bottle of rat poison next to where the arsenic bottle stood.

Next morning, you drop the fingerprints off at the police lab and head for the Thrombey house.

Turn to page 44.

You arrive at the Thrombey house about 9:00 in the morning. Since their cars are all parked in the driveway, you can tell that Robert, Angela, and Chartwell have all arrived. Prufrock must have asked them to come so that he could question them further.

You are startled by a noise behind Chartwell's car. A face appears over the hood. It's Jenny Mudge!

Beckoning you over, she says "I beat you here, and look what I found inside this car!"

Peering in the window, you can see a pair of garden shears half-hidden under the front seat.

"Interesting," you say.

"What's more interesting," says Jenny, "is that the man with the beard put them there."

"What man with a beard?"

"The one who drove up in *that* car." Jenny points at the red sports car belonging to Dr. Robert Lipscomb.

Out of the corner of your eyes you see Helga standing at the front door.

"Won't you come in?" she calls.

"Thanks," you call back. "I'll come in just a minute." You turn to thank Jenny, but she is already bicycling down the drive, waving at you over her shoulder.

Turn to page 44.

By the time you return to the house the dinner guests have left.

Jane does not object to your looking around, and you search under the refrigerator and behind the stove, then shine your flashlight outside. Something is glittering in the shrubbery. A minute later, you recover a bottle from the thick growth.

The next morning you visit Jenkins in the hospital.

"No doubt about it," he says. "That's the arsenic bottle that was in the greenhouse. I remember the way a piece of the label is torn off."

You thank Jenkins and head back to the Thrombey house.

Turn to page 44.

You find Jenny on the front porch of her house, sitting in a rocker reading a magazine. Taking a seat in an old wicker chair, you tip back and put your feet up on the porch railing.

"Well, do you have any theory about the case?" you ask.

"How's this for a theory," Jenny says. "Harlowe Thrombey committed suicide."

"But why? And why would he do it in a way that made it look like murder?" you ask.

"Maybe he was sick and tired of living," she replies, her large brown eyes fixed on you. "And he did it that way because he wanted to make Jane suffer and let his niece Angela inherit all his money!"

"Why do you think he would be such a rat?" you ask.

"Well, Helga says he always thought someone was out to get him—mainly, his wife! So, maybe he pretended he was murdered to prove that he was right!"

Jenny is smiling broadly by the time she finishes, and you begin to wonder whether she's pulling your leg. Still, her theory just might be right!

If you think Jenny's theory is not worth investigating, turn to page 45.

If you think her theory is worth investigating, turn to page 46.

You lean back and put your feet up on a table—your best thinking position—but no great ideas come to you.

The phone rings. It's Thrombey's gardener, Jenkins.

"I've been trying to reach you," he says. "There's something I couldn't bring myself to tell you before, but I don't think I should wait any longer."

"Go ahead," you reply.

"A couple of weeks ago, a man named Falcon called me and said that he knew how I could make a lot of money. He asked me to meet him at the White Horse Inn. I went there, and you can bet I was surprised when I learned that the job he had in mind was for me to murder Mr. Harlowe Thrombey! I turned and walked out of the place before I lost control and knocked his block off!"

Go on to the next page.

"Can you describe Mr. Falcon for me?" you ask.

"Not very well," Jenkins says. "He had on a tan raincoat and a hat pulled over his forehead. I don't even know what color his hair was. I only looked at him for a few seconds. He was plain looking, medium size, anywhere from thirty to forty years old."

"Was there anything special about him? Did he have a beard or a scar, for instance?"

"Nothing I noticed," Jenkins says. "Except . . . he did have *a nose like the beak of an eagle.*"

"That's something to go on," you say. "Thanks for calling."

If you decide to check the police records on any man named Falcon, turn to page 47.

If you decide to question the manager and waiters at the White Horse Inn about Mr. Falcon, turn to page 48.

If you decide to forget about Mr. Falcon for the moment and go back to the Thrombey house, turn to page 49.

Helga meets you at the front door and shows you into the library.

"Everyone else is here," she says. "Inspector Prufrock asked them to meet him in the library at nine o'clock, but he just called to say that his alarm clock didn't go off and he'll be a little late."

If you talk to Chartwell, turn to page 55.

If you talk to Robert, turn to page 58.

If you talk to Angela, turn to page 62.

If you talk to Helga, turn to page 63.

If you decide to walk around the grounds and think about the case for awhile, turn to page 64.

If Harlowe Thrombey wanted to commit
suicide, why would he have asked for your help?
It seems certain he was murdered. But you need
more evidence. Perhaps you should return to the
Thrombey house. On the other hand, maybe
Jenny has some other ideas.

---

*If you return to the Thrombey house,
turn to page 49.*

*If you talk further to Jenny,
turn to page 52.*

Did Harlowe Thrombey commit suicide? It sounds like a farfetched theory, but as a detective you must consider all the possibilities.

The best way to find out is to pay a call to Thrombey's physician, Dr. Paul Bloom. You rush to his office and then wait a long time with nothing to do but read old copies of the *Reader's Digest*. Finally, his nurse shows you into his private office.

"I'm glad you're working on the case," the doctor says. "I'll try to help if I can."

"Thanks. What I want to know is—was Harlowe Thrombey in failing health at the time of his death? Or depressed?"

"Not at all," Dr. Bloom replies. "He did seem to think someone was out to get him. Now it's clear that he had good reason to be afraid."

If what Dr. Bloom has told you is true, it's hardly likely that Thrombey took his own life.

You head over to the Thrombey house. Several cars are in the driveway, including Prufrock's. Chartwell lets you in the front door, but as soon as you step in, he hurries out, headed toward his car.

Turn to page 85.

Your search of the police records gives you a possible lead. There is no record of any man named Falcon, but one name catches your eye—that of John J. Keane, alias Henry Hawk.

The file shows that Mr. Keane has been twice convicted for bribery and once for robbery. Hawk is an odd name. The falcon and the hawk are both birds of prey. Could it be that Mr. Keane likes to use the name of a bird as an alias? Could Mr. Falcon really be Mr. Keane?

If you decide to investigate Mr. Keane, turn to page 50.

If you decide this is an unlikely theory and that you'd better return to the Thrombey house, turn to page 89.

You find a waitress at the White Horse Inn who recalls the man who sits at the table under the clock.

"I know Mr. Falcon," she tells you. "If the table under the clock is taken when he gets here, he usually waits in the lounge until it's free."

"How often does he come here?" you ask.

"Almost every day. If you stick around, you'll see him, but I thought his name was Hawk. That's the name he uses when he makes reservations. Somebody told me he's in the business of renting juke boxes. Maybe you can find out where his office is. But he'll probably be in here for lunch."

If you wait around the White Horse hoping Mr. Falcon will show up, turn to page 53.

If you try to track down Mr. Falcon at his office, turn to page 57.

When you arrive at the house a half hour later, you see a large, black car in the driveway. A short man, dressed in a gray pin-striped suit, is walking toward it. With him is Jane Thrombey.

Turn to page 79.

50

You're able to find Mr. Keane's address in the police files. He lives in a six-story apartment building. There are two apartments on each floor, and Keane occupies one on the top. By the time you get there, you're feeling very nervous. You decide to talk to the building superintendent.

"Yes, I know Keane," he says. "If you're looking for him, you came just in time. I understand he's leaving town tonight. But I don't advise you to go up there. He doesn't like visitors."

If you decide to go up and call on Mr. Keane,
turn to page 65.

If you decide to wait outside for him,
turn to page 66.

"Theories are fine," you say, "but have you found any clues?"

"You know the tall man—Harlowe Thrombey's nephew?" she says.

"Chartwell?"

"Yes, Chartwell. I saw him an hour ago standing by the door to the greenhouse—looking at it through a magnifying glass."

"Do you think he was returning to the scene of the crime?"

Jenny grins. "If he were returning to the scene of the crime, he wouldn't need a magnifying glass. He was acting more like a detective—like us!"

You think about what Jenny has told you as you walk over to the Thrombey house. The front door is open, and you walk right in.

Turn to page 85.

You spend the better part of two days waiting for Mr. Falcon to show up at the White Horse Inn. You're about ready to quit, when the manager comes up and taps you on the shoulder.

"I forgot to tell you," he says, "about that fellow you're waiting for. I hear he's left town. Just between you and me, it's gotten too hot for him around here."

You have wasted a lot of time. You must get back on the track. First you call Prufrock to find out whether he has made any progress.

"I've solved the murder of Harlowe Thrombey," says Prufrock triumphantly. "Sorry you weren't around. You might have learned something about this business!"

Go on to page 54.

"How did you solve it?"

There is no response for a moment, but you hear puffing sounds over the telephone. Prufrock must be lighting his smelly pipe. "Well," he says, "we've been watching Johnny Keane, also known as Henry Falcon, Henry Hawk, and two or three other names. He has a reputation for putting people away—for a fee. We bugged a phone call between him and Dr. Robert Lipscomb. It turns out that Robert hired Keane to knock off Harlowe Thrombey and then decided to do the job himself. We pulled Robert in and told him we knew all about him. He said that Angela did it. When we got hold of her, we soon found out they did it together: he got the poison and she poured it in the bottle. We have signed confessions from both of them!"

"Nice going," you say, as you hang up the phone. It seems incredible. While you were wasting time at the White Horse Inn, one of the worst police inspectors in the country has solved the Harlowe Thrombey murder case!

The End

You ask Chartwell to step into the music room with you so that the two of you can talk alone.

"I know people think that I resented Uncle Harlowe's success," Chartwell says. "They think I wanted to get control of Thrombey Plastics Company." He pauses a moment to pull out a handkerchief and wipe his brow. "Believe me, I would *never* have murdered him!"

"Who else would have?"

"I would be certain it's Dr. Robert Lipscomb," Chartwell says, "except that he stayed with *me* in the game room all evening."

"What about Jane?"

"She was bored with him, all right, but I can't believe she would have done this!"

"What about Angela?"

"It's strange about Angela," Chartwell says. "Uncle Harlowe was very fond of her. I'm sure she's going to inherit a good deal of his money. I used to like her, too—before she became so friendly with Robert Lipscomb."

Turn to page 59.

Looking under "Juke Boxes" in the Yellow Pages, you find a listing for *Eagle Juke Box Company*. You have a hunch that's where you'll find Mr. Falcon, alias Mr. Hawk.

A half hour later, you are in the office of its president—John Keane. A tough looking man, Keane has a plain face, except for his nose, which reminds you of the beak of an eagle. A row of juke boxes lines the walls. Keane tilts back in a chair with his feet on the desk, puffing on a cigar while he fiddles with a remote control gadget that operates the juke boxes. You soon find that, when *you* talk, he turns the volume up, and, when *he* talks, he turns the volume down.

"Let's get to the point," Keane snaps. "Thrombey's dead. He can't pay you anymore. You're looking for a new client, right? Well, you came to the right place. You have quite a reputation. We can use you."

Keane talks like a machine gun, punctuating each short sentence with a puff on his cigar.

*If you say, "What kind of job
do you have in mind?"
turn to page 67.*

*If you say, "Look, I'm not here to work for you.
I want you to answer a few questions,"
turn to page 68.*

"I've already talked to the police," Robert snaps at you. "Chartwell and I were in the game room all evening. I've told everybody— Thrombey's dying words were *'Jane did it.'* Now leave me alone!"

"But during the afternoon, didn't you make a little tour of the grounds?" you persist.

"No! I spent the entire time in the library," he replies. "I had several very important calls to make, and I have some more to make right now!"

Robert walks off without another word, leaving you wondering what to do next.

Turn to page 59.

Glancing out the window, you notice Prufrock's car in the driveway. You don't feel like talking to him right now so you decide to return home and give the case some more thought.

As you walk in your front door it occurs to you that it might be a good idea to join forces with Jenny Mudge.

If you call Jenny, turn to page 60.

If not, turn to page 42.

60

Jenny is glad to hear from you. "I agree that the best way to solve this case is to work together," she says. "You know more about it than I do, except that I know Helga pretty well, and I'm certain that she would never have done it. Besides, she and I were in the kitchen when the murderer broke into the greenhouse. I know, because the greenhouse was locked when I came to visit about 4:30, but when I started home at about 6:00 I noticed it was broken open."

"I don't think it could be Jenkins," you say. "He was in the hospital the whole time."

"Who do you think *is* the most likely suspect then?" Jenny asks. "Let me know and I'll trail whoever it is."

If you ask Jenny to trail:

Chartwell, turn to page 70.
Robert, turn to page 71.
Jane, turn to page 72.
Angela, turn to page 73.

62

You usher Angela into the music room so you can talk with her alone. She looks unsmilingly into your eyes. Something about her reminds you of a cat—sleek, clever and unpredictable.

"You arrived last night at about seven. What were you doing during the two hours before that?" you ask.

"I was at my dentist, Dr. Marlowe, in Springdale," she replies. "It's an hour's drive. My appointment was at 5:00. I was there an hour, and it took me an hour to get here."

"Did you go to the pantry at all after I left you and Jane in the music room at 8:30?"

"No! Jane and I played piano duets, but then she left the room a short while after you did!"

"One more question—what is your relationship with Dr. Robert Lipscomb?"

"There's been talk that we might get married, but we are just friends."

Glancing out the window, you notice a large black car pulling up the drive. Jane Thrombey gets out. With her is a man wearing a dark gray pin-striped suit. Prufrock's car is there too. He must have arrived while you were talking to Angela.

If you decide to talk to Chartwell, turn to page 74.

If you decide to talk to Inspector Prufrock, turn to page 75.

If you decide to go outside and talk to Jane, turn to page 79.

You ask Helga to sit with you in the dining room. She seems frightened, and you try to reassure her that there is nothing to fear.

"I just want to ask you a few questions," you say. "First of all, where were you from the time you cleared off the dinner dishes until the time Mr. Thrombey died?"

"I left immediately for the hospital."

"When did you arrive?"

"About 8:30."

After thanking Helga, you call the hospital to find out who the floor nurse was during visiting hours the previous evening. A second call brings you the information you need: Helga did visit her brother the night before, arriving at 8:30 just as she said.

As you hang up the phone, you glance out the window, where you see Jane Thrombey, accompanied by a man dressed in a gray pin-striped suit.

Turn to page 79.

Deciding you can probably think more clearly while taking a walk than by sitting in the musty house, you step outside and stroll through the gardens.

As you approach the greenhouse you are surprised to see Jenny Mudge standing by the door. She is measuring something with a ruler.

"Look!" she calls to you. "They match!"

"What?"

"The marks where the door was pried open match the points of the shears Robert Lipscomb put in Chartwell's car!"

Jenny starts across the lawn—headed home. "What do you make of that?" she calls over her shoulder.

You walk back toward the entrance to the house. Several cars are parked in the driveway, including Prufrock's. Chartwell lets you in the front door, but as soon as you step in he hurries out, headed toward his car.

Turn to page 85.

You take the tiny elevator up to the sixth floor and pause a moment in the shabby, dimly lit hallway between the two doors marked 6A and 6B.

You knock on Keane's door. In a moment it opens. Facing you is a medium-sized, middle-aged man with a nose like an eagle's beak. He glares at you a moment, sizing you up with mean, narrowed eyes.

"Who are you?" he asks gruffly.

If you say, "I'm investigating the murder of Harlowe Thrombey and I would like to ask a few questions," turn to page 80.

If you say, "I hear you're a real pro and I have a good piece of business for you," turn to page 81.

If Keane is a criminal, it would be foolish to knock on his door just as he is about to get out of town. You'll learn more about him if he doesn't know you are on his trail.

Capping your head with a wig of curly gray hair from your disguise kit, you take a seat on the front steps of a nearby house and pretend to read a newspaper.

A red sports car pulls up, and a trim, bearded man steps out. He hurries into Keane's apartment building. It's Dr. Robert Lipscomb!

You jump out and peer into his car. There is a piece of notepaper on the front seat. Keane's name and address are scrawled on it, and also the words "TWA Flight 40 at 4:15."

You cross the street to a pay phone, call Prufrock and tell him what you've discovered. While you're still talking, Keane and Robert come out of the building and get into Robert's car.

"Johnny Keane is a hit man," Prufrock says. "There's only one reason Robert would visit him—to pay him off for keeping quiet! I'll have my men ready at the airport to meet them. You've given me all the information I need to solve the Harlowe Thrombey murder case."

You wait for Prufrock to thank you for your work, but that's not his way.

The End

"I have a friend I don't like anymore," Keane says. "Dr. Robert Lipscomb. He hired me to do a job for him and then decided to take care of it himself. Now he and his girlfriend are coming into a lot of money for knocking off her uncle. I want you to warn them that half of their take belongs to me. Got me?"

"Got you," you reply. "What's in it for me?"

"Ten percent."

"It's a deal."

You leave Keane and immediately head over to the office of Inspector Prufrock. When you tell him of your conversation with Keane, Prufock jumps out of his car, his eyes glistening with excitement.

"I knew it was them," he says. "I'll have them behind bars in a few weeks."

For once, Prufrock is as good as his word. Robert and Angela are tried and convicted for the murder of Harlowe Thrombey.

Soon afterward, you receive a letter from Jane Thrombey. It is a note of thanks for solving the Harlowe Thrombey murder case, and with it is a check for $5,000.

The End

"Sure," Keane says, "I'd answer all your questions, except that I don't think the answers would do you any good. . . ."

He turns up the volume so high it hurts your ears. The door opens, revealing a thick-set man with huge hands and dull gray eyes. He stands gaping at you for a moment and then starts walking slowly toward you.

You race toward the door. He lunges at you, but you duck under his massive arms and dart out the door. You run out of the building and down the street at top speed, slowing only when you're sure no one is following.

You've almost reached home when you hear a car screeching to a stop. Turning, you get a glimpse of a masked figure before you feel a smashing blow on your head. Then everything goes blank.

Sometime later, you come to. Your head is throbbing. One of your legs is in a cast, suspended in a sling. A doctor is looking down at you, shaking his head.

"You're going to be out of action for a few weeks," he says, "but you'll be O.K."

"Thanks," you say. "I have a lot of work to do."

"Not on the Harlowe Thrombey murder case," the doctor says. "I hear it's been solved by someone you may know—a girl named Jenny Mudge. They says she's the smartest detective around."

The End

"I think you should watch Thrombey's nephew, Chartwell," you tell Jenny. "It's possible he pried open the greenhouse door and took the arsenic. If so, he may return to make sure he didn't leave any clues. Also since he and Dr. Robert Lipscomb both say they were in the game room together before the murder, I'd be interested to know whether they are having any meetings now."

Turn to page 89.

"I'm most suspicious of Dr. Robert Lipscomb," you tell Jenny. "I'm curious to know about his relationship with Angela. She says they are just friends, but I'm not so sure."

"I'm on my way," Jenny says.

Turn to page 89.

"I'd like you to watch Jane Thrombey," you tell Jenny. "Harlowe Thrombey thought she might be out to get him, and maybe she was. She knew where the arsenic was kept. She might have given it to one of the others. If she was conspiring with someone, she will probably meet with that person again."

"O.K." Jenny replies.

Turn to page 89.

"I'd like you to watch Angela," you tell Jenny.
"Find out what her habits are, and where she was
the afternoon of the murder. She must have
known where the arsenic was."

"O.K.," says Jenny.

Turn to page 89.

"I can talk only a few minutes," Chartwell says.

"I have only a few questions," you reply. "First, how long was it before he screamed that Harlowe Thrombey left you and Robert in the game room?"

"It couldn't have been more than five minutes," Chartwell replies.

"Who knew that arsenic was kept in the greenhouse?"

"Everyone but Dr. Robert Lipscomb, but I'll tell you I'm very suspicious of that fellow."

"Where were you between the time you arrived the afternoon of the murder and the time we first met?"

"Why, I met you as soon as I arrived at the house. But you should know that when I pulled up the drive I saw Robert running to the front door—coming from the direction of the greenhouse. I think he was the one who broke in and took the arsenic."

Chartwell glances at his watch, turns and heads out the door. At the same time . . .

Turn to page 85.

"I have been giving this case a lot of thought," Prufrock tells you. "It's odd that you were walking around the house freely while the other guests were busy. *You* are the one who could most easily have committed the crime."

You start to protest, but Prufrock obviously wants to do all the talking. "Of course," he continues, "you would be the *last* one I would suspect. I would be *astounded* if *you* turned out to be the murderer. But, if everyone else were logically excluded, that would, of course, mean that you were guilty! *Now get out of here—you're interfering with my work!*

Prufrock waves you away, and you're glad to leave. Of course he doesn't *really* suspect you. At least you hope not. But he's such an idiot, it's sometimes hard to know what he's thinking!

You return home, where you are surprised to find that someone has left a note outside your door. It says:

> I have some important evidence
> for you. Meet me at the White
> Horse Inn at five o'clock.
> I'll be sitting under the clock.
>   Henry Falcon

Go on to page 77.

Half an hour later you walk up to the neatly dressed man sitting under the clock in the lobby of the White Horse Inn. He rises to meet you and points toward a chair. You can't help staring for a moment at his hawklike nose.

"Falcon's the name," he says. "Have a seat. I didn't want to go to the police about this, but when I heard you were involved, I decided I should talk to you."

"Please do," you reply.

"A few days ago, I was walking down Hope Street and picked this up. It was already opened."

He hands you a letter addressed to a Mr. Richard Kent, Hope Street. Printed on the top is Jane Thrombey's name and address. It reads:

> *Dearest Richard,*
> *I think of you every hour. Harlowe will be out of the way in only a few days. I will call you as soon as the deed is done. Love forever.*
> *Jane*

Go on to page 78.

"I couldn't decide what to do," Falcon continues. "Then I read in the newspaper that Harlowe Thrombey had been murdered. I didn't want to be involved, but I felt I had to do something, so I called you."

"I'm glad you did," you reply. "Tell me, did you ever know either Mrs. Thrombey or Mr. Kent?"

"Never."

You thank Falcon for his help and tell him you will follow up on the letter.

If you decide to investigate the letter and telephone Jane Thrombey, turn to page 83.

If you feel that the letter is a false lead and decide to return to the Thrombey house, turn to page 89.

If you decide that the letter proves that Jane is the murderer, turn to page 103.

You go out to talk to Jane, but the man in the pin-striped suit steps in front of her.

"I'm Mr. Prem," he says, "Mrs. Thrombey's lawyer."

"Can you tell me, Mr. Prem," you ask, "who will inherit all of Harlowe Thrombey's money?"

Prem smiles. "Yes, but it will not help you solve this case, I'm afraid. Thrombey's will provides that his fortune will be divided equally among his wife, Jane; his niece, Angela; and his nephew, Chartwell. Of course, under the law, a murderer is not allowed to inherit anything from the person he or she murders!"

"If caught," you say.

"If caught." Prem turns his back. "I think we'd better return to my office," he says to Jane.

You go on into the Thrombey house, almost bumping into Chartwell as you step inside the front door. This looks like a good time to question him.

Turn to page 74.

"Oh, yeah," Keane says in an almost friendly tone of voice. "Won't you come in?"

You step inside and he shuts the door behind you. The room is empty except for a couple of suitcases, a battered desk, and a ragged old sofa.

"Excuse me while I finish getting dressed. I'm just about to leave," Keane says. "You're a real good detective, catching up with me just like that. You really got on to me, didn't you?"

Keane picks up a jacket draped over the sofa. As he slips it on, you notice something bulging from the inside pocket. He stares at you with a crazed look. You begin to drift toward the door. But Keane is fast; he pulls out an automatic, taking time only to say—*"Too good"* before letting you have it.

The End

"Yeah, come in," Keane says.

You decide the best way to get information from Keane is to play along with him. "I've heard about you," you say. "There's someone who's been giving me a lot of trouble, and I think you're the one who could take care of him for me. That would be worth a lot to me."

"What are you talking about?" Keane asks. "What makes you think I do that kind of thing?" There is something in Keane's tone that suggests you are on the right track.

"Well," you reply, "I heard you arranged things with Harlowe Thrombey, who passed away just the other day."

"You have big ears," Keane says in a mocking tone of voice. Then he adds, "The truth is I didn't pull that one off. Not that I didn't try," he laughs. "But the guy who hired me didn't give me enough time—he was so anxious to get the job done—so I said, 'You're the doctor!' " He laughs again.

"Dr. Robert Lipscomb? Well, he did a pretty good job of it," you say.

"Yes . . ." Keane says. "He's the kind of man I like, but the one I really admire is his girlfriend Angela. She was the one who really got the job done."

While Keane talks, you edge toward a battered desk in the corner of the room. Keane seems to have forgotten that he left a snub-nosed .28 pistol on it.

Go on to page 82.

A moment later his ugly face turns pale as you grab the pistol and level it at him. Keeping him covered, you ease across the room and pick up the phone.

"Inspector Prufrock," you say a moment later. "I have a man here who can tell you all you need to know about the Harlowe Thrombey murder case."

The End

You telephone Jane Thrombey. Helga answers. She tells you that Jane went to visit her lawyer, Mr. Gilliam Prem. You go to his office at once, but find him unwilling to talk—until you tell him you have evidence that may prove his client guilty of murder.

You hand Prem the letter. He glances at it and scowls. "I don't know where you got this, but it's a fake," he says. "Jane has a friend named Richard Kent, but he's been in Japan on business for the past month. Besides, I'm an expert, and I know Jane's signature. What you have there is a childish forgery!"

If you decide to find your own expert, turn to page 92.

If you decide to turn the letter over to Prufrock, turn to page 93.

Prufrock strides toward you from the direction of the library. "I've solved the murder!" he shouts.

Through the window you see Chartwell getting into his car.

"How interesting," you say. "Who is it?"

"You may have heard that the murderer poured arsenic into Thrombey's brandy bottle late in the evening. We found that Chartwell broke into the greenhouse, using a pair of garden shears to pry the door open. We found the shears in his car. The blade points match the marks made when the murderer pried the padlock off the greenhouse door."

"I wouldn't be so sure of yourself, Prufrock," you say.

The two of you look out the window as Chartwell's car roars down the drive.

"Whose car is that?" Prufrock demands.

"I'm afraid it belongs to the man you want to arrest," you reply.

Prufrock rushes outdoors. You follow and watch him as he races to his car and jumps behind the wheel, fumbling for his keys.

"WHERE ARE THE KEYS TO THIS CAR?" he yells.

A policeman rushes from the house, holding a set of keys up in the air. "You told me never to leave them in the car, sir," he calls, as he runs toward the car.

A moment later they roar down the drive, lights flashing and siren screaming.

Go on to page 86.

You shake your head in disbelief. It's at least as likely that the person who used the shears would toss them into Chartwell's car as that Chartwell would leave them there. Prufrock reminds you of a dog chasing a rabbit that has just run the other way.

Turn to page 89.

Reaching for your blindfold, you feel a smashing pain in your head. . . .

You are slowly waking up. Your head is pounding. A bandage covers half your scalp and one ear. You're lying somewhere—it must be a hospital bed. A doctor is standing next to you.

"We had to stitch you up a little," he says. "It's not serious; you can walk out of here in the morning."

He starts to leave and then turns back. "Oh, they found this note next to you."

He hands you an envelope from which you remove a small sheet of yellow-ruled paper; it reads:

> *Drop this case or next time you'll end up*
> *in the cemetery.*

In this business you have to take chances. Still, it might be healthier to solve this case in a hurry.

Early the next morning, you walk out of the hospital into the bright sunshine, thinking about Angela. Was she the one who broke into the greenhouse, took the arsenic, and poisoned the brandy?

If you investigate Angela, turn to page 94.

If you decide it might be a good idea to check with Jenny Mudge, turn to page 95.

You return home, for you have some work to do there before lunch. By the time you get back to the Thrombey house, no one seems to be at home. After ringing the bell several times you try the door. It's unlocked, and you step inside and walk down the hall to the library. Suddenly you feel the hard pressure of a gun in your back!

"Don't move. Don't look around." A heavy hand on your shoulder shoves you into a chair. You dare not resist as your attacker wraps a towel tightly around your head and over your eyes and ties you to a chair.

You hear papers rustling. Someone must be searching through Harlowe Thrombey's desk. You could probably get a hand free and rip off your blindfold, but that might be dangerous.

If you try to rip off your blindfold, turn to page 87.

If you sit quietly, turn to page 90.

You sit quietly and listen to the sound of desk drawers sliding open and shut, then something crashing to the floor.

You hear a cry—and a voice you recognize. You rip off the blindfold. There, in the dim light, hands raised in the air, is Dr. Robert Lipscomb. A policeman is right behind him, gun in hand. Standing a few feet away, a big smile on her face, is Jenny Mudge!

You hear a police siren outside. A minute later, Inspector Prufrock storms into the room. Right behind him are Jane, Angela, and Chartwell, followed by two more policemen.

"I was questioning them all down at headquarters when I heard what was going on out here. Now we'll get to the bottom of this!" Prufrock says. In a flash, he snaps a pair of handcuffs on Robert.

"I'm innocent!" Robert cries. "Chartwell will tell you that I couldn't have poisoned Harlowe. We were together in the game room all evening! Jane is the one who did it! As I've told everyone—Harlowe Thrombey accused her in his dying words!"

Turn to page 121.

It's not surprising that Gilliam Prem claims the letter is a forgery. As Jane's lawyer, he is paid to protect her! You need an opinion you can trust. Fortunately, you have the name of a handwriting expert, Marie Furno. You quickly get hold of her on the phone.

"Come over to my house any time," Marie says. "Be sure to get a true example of Jane Thrombey's signature so I can compare it with the one on the letter you have."

You're in good luck. Helga is able to supply you with a sample of Jane's signature. A half hour later you are standing next to Marie Furno while she peers through a magnifying glass. She looks up at you, a smile on her face.

"Gilliam Prem was wrong when he said this was a childish forgery," she says. "It's a very clever forgery!"

"Thanks," you reply. "It looks like someone wanted to frame her."

"I'm sure you'll find out who it is," Marie says.

If you think you have the case solved, turn to page 105.

If not, turn to page 101.

You deliver the letter to Prufrock and he agrees to have his handwriting expert examine it.

An hour later, you call to find out the results.

"I'm sorry, but we had a little accident here," says Prufrock.

"What sort of accident?"

"It's one of those things that sometimes happens, even in the best organizations."

"What happened?"

"I'm afraid one of our people spilled a pot of coffee on the letter and now we can't read anything.

You hang up in disgust. As usual, there's no use expecting help from Prufrock.

Turn to page 101.

You are curious about Angela's visit to Dr. Marlowe, her dentist, the afternoon of the murder, and you decide to pay a visit to his office.

"I'm checking something for the Thrombey family," you tell the nurse. "Was Harlowe Thrombey's niece, Angela, here two days ago from 5:00 to 6:00?"

"Why yes, that's right," the nurse replies. "Did she leave something here?"

"No, I'm just checking. What was she here for? What treatment?"

"She was just getting her teeth cleaned," the nurse replies. "She called to make the appointment the day before, and, when I said we were all booked up, she insisted on coming at five o'clock, anyway. Can you imagine that? She's just lucky Dr. Marlowe was able to take her."

Turn to page 101.

You waste no time in phoning Jenny.

If you asked Jenny to watch:

> *Robert, turn to page 97.*
> *Chartwell, turn to page 98.*
> *Jane, turn to page 99.*
> *Angela, turn to page 100.*

If you didn't ask her to watch anyone,
> *turn to page 96.*

Jenny's father answers the phone. "She's out," he says. "I don't expect her back until late this afternoon."

You'll have to continue the investigation without her for a while.

Turn to page 101.

Jenny's father answers. "She's not home," he says. "But she just phoned from police headquarters. The case is solved! In fact, it was Jenny who solved it!"

"How?" you ask.

"Jenny said it was so easy it was hardly any fun. She sat behind Robert and Angela in the movies and heard them whispering about how they had committed the perfect crime!"

The End

"Funny thing about Chartwell," Jenny says. "He acts as if *he* is the detective. He spends a lot of time at the greenhouse, snooping around the door with a magnifying glass. I couldn't get close enough to see what he was looking for, but . . . in my opinion he's harmless."

"Thanks, Jenny," you say. "I'll talk to you later."

Turn to page 101.

"Sorry," Jenny says, "I wasn't able to find out much about Jane. Her lawyer came to visit a couple of times. I guess she's pretty worried."

"I guess so," you reply, "but with someone like Prufrock in charge of the case, you could be worried even if you're innocent!"

Turn to page 101.

"I've been watching Angela like a hawk," Jenny says. "But she hasn't been doing a thing—except playing the piano. She's been practicing all day long. I taped it on my cassette recorder and played it to my music teacher. It's called *Moonlight Sonata*, by Beethoven. My music teacher says that Angela is just a beginner."

"Thanks, Jenny," you say. "That could be important."

Turn to page 101.

WHAT SHOULD YOU DO NEXT?

If you found fingerprints on the bottle of brandy and you want to check out the lab report, turn to page 106.

If you found fingerprints in the greenhouse and want to check out the lab report, turn to page 110.

If you decide to talk to:
Robert, turn to page 107.
Chartwell, turn to page 111.
Angela, turn to page 112.
Jane, turn to page 114.
Jenny, turn to page 115.
Inspector Prufrock, turn to page 116.
Gilliam Prem, turn to page 117.

If you decide to just sit in a quiet place and think about what you already know, turn to page 118.

If you decide to give up on the case, turn to page 119.

If you're absolutely sure you have the case wrapped up, turn to page 122.

A few minutes later you reach Prufrock on the phone.

"Well, what is it?" he says.

"Just the solution to the Harlowe Thrombey murder case," you reply. "I have a letter signed by Jane Thrombey which is as good as a confession of the crime."

Prufrock asks you to come to police headquarters. When you arrive, he takes the letter and says he will be back in a few minutes. Half an hour goes by while you pace back and forth wondering why you always have to do Prufrock's work for him. Finally he returns—a broad grin on his face.

"Our handwriting expert says that this letter is a forgery. I'm not surprised, of course, because the Harlowe Thrombey murder case has already been solved—by a friend of yours, I believe. Jenny Mudge is her name."

"Who did it? How was it solved?" you ask.

"Thrombey's niece, Angela, did it," says Prufrock. "And Jenny solved it by *not* finding fingerprints!"

"How can you solve a case by not finding fingerprints?"

Go on to page 104.

"Very simple," says Prufrock. "Angela claimed that she continued to play the small piano after Jane left the room. Jenny checked for fingerprints on the piano keys. If Angela had played it, she would have left some prints, at least smudged prints, but there were none at all. When we told Angela this, she got very shaken. Finally, she confessed that Robert Lipscomb broke into the greenhouse and got the arsenic, and that she was the one who poured it into Thrombey's bottle of brandy!"

The End

A few minutes later you walk into Prufrock's office and hand him the letter.

"This proves Jane did it!" he exclaims.

"Just the opposite," you reply. "This letter is a forgery. If someone is trying to frame her, it means she *didn't* do it. Therefore, Robert was lying when he said that Harlowe Thrombey accused Jane just before he died."

"But Robert couldn't have poured the poison into the brandy bottle," Prufrock insists. "Chartwell admitted that Robert stayed in the game room all evening, and I know that Chartwell wouldn't protect Robert; in fact Chartwell accused Robert of breaking into the greenhouse!"

"Robert didn't have to poison the brandy bottle," you say. "He gave the poison to Angela, and *she* poured it into the brandy bottle."

Prufrock scratches his head a moment. "Well, how do you know Robert didn't give the poison to Jane?"

"If he had," you reply, "he wouldn't have said that Thrombey accused Jane in his dying words, because then Jane would have blamed Robert for getting the poison for her!"

Prufrock shakes his head in amazement. Suddenly, he stalks off.

"Where are you going?" you call after him.

"To get a warrant for the arrest of Angela and Robert for the murder of Harlowe Thrombey!"

Among his other faults, Prufrock doesn't know how to say "thank you."

The End

The lab report identifies the prints on the brandy bottle as belonging to Harlowe Thrombey.

Try another lead.
Turn back to page 101.

You telephone Robert Lipscomb and he agrees to meet you at the Thrombey house in half an hour. You get Prufrock on the phone and ask him to come, too.

"I can't," he replies. "I'm questioning the other suspects right now."

"Bring them along," you say, "and I promise to wrap this case up today."

There is a long pause before Prufrock answers. "O.K. But if you don't deliver on that promise, I'll arrest you for interfering with the work of a police officer!"

A half hour later the library is filled with people. Jane, Chartwell, and Angela are seated along one wall, while Robert Lipscomb sits in a high-backed armchair. You stand in a corner where you can watch everyone at once. Prufrock and another policeman stay near the door.

"All right, Sherlock Holmes," Prufrock says, blowing a puff of pipe smoke in your direction. "Tell us how Harlowe Thrombey was murdered."

"Robert can tell us best," you reply.

"Of course I can," Robert says, "because I was the one who heard Harlowe Thrombey's last words—'*Jane poured my last drink.*'"

Go on to the next page.

Turn to page 121.

The lab report identifies most of the prints in the greenhouse as belonging to Jenkins, the gardener. But a set of prints found on a can of paint belong to Jane Thrombey, thumb and finger-prints on the bottle of rat poison belong to Dr. Robert Lipscomb, and a set of prints on a magnifying glass are identified as Chartwell's.

This lab report tells you something, but you need more information to solve the murder.

Turn back to page 101.

You find Chartwell in an angry mood.

"Prufrock now says I pried the greenhouse open when I stopped by the morning of the murder to return a book. But I know Robert did it. I saw him running into the house just as I was arriving for dinner."

If you think it would be worthwhile talking to one of the other suspects, turn to page 101.

If you decide to give up on the case, turn to page 119.

If you're absolutely sure you've solved the murder, turn to page 122.

"I hope you are going to live up to your reputation by solving this case quickly," Angela says.

"I guess at least one person doesn't want me to," you reply.

"Since *I* do," Angela says, "I'll give you some help: Robert and Chartwell, much as they dislike each other, both say the other remained in the game room during the time when the murderer poisoned Uncle Harlowe's brandy bottle. I'm sure you have already found out that I was at the dentist during the time when the murderer took the arsenic from the greenhouse. So, as a matter of logic . . ."

"The murderer must be Jane?" you ask.

Angela smiles.

"Your skills at logic are so good," you continue, *"but I know that Jane, not you, was playing the piano during the time when the brandy was poisoned."*

Angela looks at you wide-eyed.

"But you don't!" she cries. "Perhaps you *thought* it was Jane playing the whole time. You didn't realize that when she left, I played for ten or fifteen minutes."

"Beethoven?" you ask.

"Yes, as a matter of fact, it was," Angela replies coolly—*"The Moonlight Sonata."*

"Then you will be glad to demonstrate on the piano in front of a music teacher!"

Angela's face flushes with anger.

"But I couldn't have broken into the greenhouse and gotten the arsenic," she cries. "I can prove I was at the dentist!"

"I know that," you reply. "Robert tried to protect you by claiming that Harlowe Thrombey accused Jane of poisoning him. That's how I know that *he* was the one who broke into the greenhouse and got the arsenic for you."

"That fool," Angela cries. "Why did I get mixed up with that man!"

"I'm afraid you'll have a long time to think about that," you reply.

"I'm afraid you won't have a long time to think about anything," Angela says, as she levels a snub-nosed .45 at you. You realize, too late, that you have ignored an important rule for detectives: never trust a murderer.

The End

114

You find Jane Thrombey seated at the piano. She insists that on the night of the murder she was playing the piano the entire time between 8:00 and 9:00 and that it was Angela who left the room. She also says that Angela never once played the piano all evening.

If you think it would be worthwhile talking more to one of the other suspects, turn to page 101.

If you decide to give up on the case, turn to page 119.

If you're absolutely sure you've solved the murder, turn to page 122.

You find Jenny sitting on her porch, reading a Sherlock Holmes story.

"I'm glad you stopped by," she says. "I believe I've solved the case."

"Let's have it," you say.

"I was really lucky. I happened to be watching when Robert Lipscomb put a pair of garden shears in Chartwell's car. After Robert left, I borrowed the shears just long enough to see if the pointed blades matched the holes in the wood that were made when the door was pried open. They did, and that made me sure that Robert was the one who broke in and took the bottle of arsenic. . . ."

"But he couldn't have poured it into Harlowe Thrombey's brandy bottle," you say, "because Chartwell admits that Robert never left the game room. Chartwell wouldn't try to protect Robert."

"True," Jenny says. "Robert didn't pour poison into the brandy. He gave it to Angela, and she poured it!"

"Angela, and not Jane?"

"If he had given it to Jane, he wouldn't have claimed that Harlowe Thrombey *accused* Jane. Therefore, Robert must have given the arsenic bottle to Angela."

"Exactly my conclusion," you reply. "He tried to protect himself by framing Chartwell and Jane, and that was how he proved himself guilty!"

"Right!" Jenny says.

"You're a pretty good detective," you tell her.

"You're no slouch," says she. "Let's be partners!"

The End

Prufrock ushers you into his office.

"Well, what have you found?" you ask.

"This case is an unusually difficult one," he replies. "The murderer has been very clever in covering his tracks, but, as usual in these cases, I can solve it by using logic."

"Tell me," you say.

Prufrock gestures at you with his long pipe. "It could not have been Jenkins or his sister Helga, because they were in the hospital between 8:00 and 9:00—when the murderer put the arsenic in the bottle of brandy. It could not have been Jane, because she was playing in a concert when the murderer broke into the greenhouse. And it could not have been Angela. She was at the dentist's at the time of the break-in. It could not have been Chartwell, or Robert, because each says the other never left the game room after dinner."

"But, inspector, you have eliminated everybody!" you interrupt.

"Perhaps," Prufrock replies, "but as you can see, I am *very* close to a solution!"

You have trouble not laughing until you are outside Prufrock's office.

If you think it would be worthwhile talking more to one of the other suspects, turn to page 101.

If you decide to give up on the case, turn to page 119.

If you're sure you've solved the murder, turn to page 122.

"Very well, I'll talk to you," Gilliam Prem snaps at you over the phone.

"Isn't it possible Jane Thrombey poured poison into the brandy bottle, Mr. Prem?"

Prem rattles off his answer like a computer print-out. "She was playing the piano when the murderer poured arsenic into Thrombey's bottle of brandy—Beethoven's *Moonlight Sonata*. It was Angela who left the room. Angela can't play Beethoven. She's just a beginner!"

You need more information than this.
Turn back to page 101.

There is a time in every case when it is wise to stop and review what you know and put the pieces together. One thing bothers you: Chartwell and Robert each say that they both remained in the game room from 8:00 to 9:00 the night of the murder. If so, neither of them could have put arsenic in Harlowe Thrombey's brandy. Of course, it's possible that they were protecting each other, but, if they were, why would Chartwell say that he thinks Robert is guilty?

If you think it would be worthwhile talking more to one of the other suspects, turn to page 101.

If you decide to give up on the case, turn to page 119.

If you're sure you've solved the murder, turn to page 122.

It's depressing. There's nothing you hate more than not being able to solve a murder case.

The End

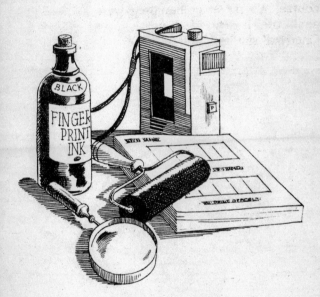

You pull your tape cassette out of your pocket and shove it in front of Robert's face.

"I had a tape recorder planted in the music room all evening!" you say. "The piano never stopped. Since Jane was the only one playing, I know you lied about Thrombey's last words!"

"But I couldn't have poured his last drink. I was in the game room!" Robert says.

"True enough," you say, "and so was Chartwell. Angela was the only one who could have put the poison in the brandy bottle."

"Then I'm innocent!" Robert cries.

"No, you're not!" screams Angela, her face red with anger. "*You* got that arsenic from the greenhouse for me!"

Suddenly, Robert is on his feet, making a break for the door. In a flash Prufrock pins him against the bookcase.

Angela slumps in her chair, burying her head in her arms.

"It's such a shame," Jane Thrombey says. "Harlowe was going to give the two of you a trip to Hawaii for a wedding present."

Prufrock shuffles toward you, takes the cassette out of your hand and stares at it dumbly like a dog staring at its reflection in the water.

"How did you think of putting a tape recorder in the music room?" he says.

"To tell the truth, I didn't," you reply, taking the cassette back from him. "This is just an old Beatles recording."

The End

You return home and dial Prufrock's special number at Police Headquarters.

"Inspector Prufrock," you say with satisfaction, "if you have a moment, I'll be glad to tell you exactly how Harlowe Thrombey was murdered."

The End

ABOUT THE AUTHOR

A graduate of Princeton University and Columbia Law School, EDWARD PACKARD lives in New York City, where he is a practicing lawyer. Mr. Packard conceived of the idea for the Choose Your Own Adventure® series in the course of telling bedtime stories to his children, Caroline, Andrea, and Wells.

ABOUT THE ILLUSTRATOR

PAUL GRANGER is a prize-winning illustrator and painter.

CHOOSE YOUR OWN ADVENTURE®

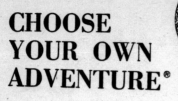

You'll want all the books in the exciting *Choose Your Own Adventure®* series offering you hundreds of fantasy adventures without ever leaving your chair. Each book takes you through an adventure—under the sea, in a space colony, on a volcanic island—in which you become the main character. What happens next in the story depends on the choices *you* make and *only you* can decide how the story ends!

☐	23228	THE CAVE OF TIME #1 Edward Packard	$1.95
☐	23229	JOURNEY UNDER THE SEA #2 R. A. Montgomery	$1.95
☐	23183	BY BALLOON TO THE SAHARA #3 D. Terman	$1.95
☐	23180	SPACE AND BEYOND #4 R. A. Montgomery	$1.95
☐	23184	THE MYSTERY OF CHIMNEY ROCK #5 Edward Packard	$1.95
☐	23182	YOUR CODE NAME IS JONAH #6 Edward Packard	$1.95
☐	23185	THE THIRD PLANET FROM ALTAIR #7 Edward Packard	$1.95
☐	23230	DEADWOOD CITY #8 Edward Packard	$1.95
☐	23181	WHO KILLED HARLOWE THROMBEY? #9 Edward Packard	$1.95
☐	23231	THE LOST JEWELS OF NABOOTI #10 R. A. Montgomery	$1.95
☐	23186	MYSTERY OF THE MAYA #11 R. A. Montgomery	$1.95
☐	23175	INSIDE UFO 54-40 #12 Edward Packard	$1.95
☐	20529	THE ABOMINABLE SNOWMAN #13 R. A. Montgomery	$1.75
☐	22515	THE FORBIDDEN CASTLE #14 Edward Packard	$1.75
☐	22541	HOUSE OF DANGER #15 R. A. Montgomery	$1.95